Doodle and the Go-cart

By the same author

Simon and the Game of Chance
Joey's Cat
Renfroe's Christmas
Queenie Peavy
D. J.'s Worst Enemy
Skinny
Tyler, Wilkin, and Skee
A Funny Place to Live

Illustrated by Alan Tiegreen

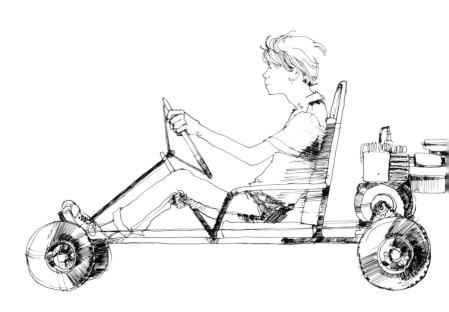

DOODLE
AND THE
GO-CART

Robert Burch

THE VIKING PRESS   NEW YORK

For Jan Cole

Contents

The
Rides at
the Party

Doodle saw a go-cart on the Fourth of July. It was the first one he had ever seen, and he knew at once that he had to have one. "How much would you say it cost?" he asked his cousin Glenn Carter.

"More than you've got," answered Glenn, heading toward the swimming pool. "And more than you'll get!"

The party was at the Moreland estate on the outskirts of Ripley, Georgia. Elsie Moreland had been in the fifth grade last year, and everyone from her homeroom had been invited to the party. Some, like Doodle's cousin Glenn, lived in town; others lived out in the country.

The go-cart belonged to Elsie's brother Donald, who was visiting Mrs. Moreland's people in Ohio. Mr.

Moreland had brought the cart from under the garage and was letting the visitors take turns in it. All the boys had ridden it at least once. A few of the girls had ridden it, but mostly they wanted to ride Duchess Rose, Elsie's registered quarter horse. Some of the boys rode the horse too.

After a while nearly all the guests had gone back to the pool. It was a swimming party, the rides being a bonus, and everyone wore a bathing suit—except Duchess Rose, of course. She wore a hand-tooled leather saddle, trimmed with turquoise, that the Morelands had brought back from their trip to Mexico.

At the end of each ride in the go-cart, Doodle got in line for another turn. He lived out in the country and could swim or go horseback riding anytime. Well, it wasn't exactly a horse he could ride at home; it was the mule, Addie Flowers. And Doodle didn't have a hand-tooled saddle studded with turquoise. In fact, he didn't have a saddle of any sort, but he could throw a burlap bag over Addie's back, tie a rope to her halter, and ride off in any direction he chose—or any direction Addie Flowers chose. And he could go swimming at home too—not in a pool, with water so clear he could see all the way to the bottom, but in the Flint River, which ran along the edge of his father's farm. It was so muddy that most of the time he couldn't see anything in it. Whenever Doodle swam there, he never knew when sticks or pine cones would brush against him, scaring him half out of the water. Still, he could swim in the river. But there was nowhere else he could enjoy a go-cart, and so he kept riding the one at the party. He and Luke Stinson were the only ones still playing with it when Mr. Moreland said, "Maybe we'd better put it away now. It's time to roll out the barbecue grill and get a fire started for the hamburgers."

Luke ran over to the pool, yelling to Andy Hill to throw him the beach ball that the boys were keeping away from the girls. When Andy threw it to Glenn instead, Luke did a bellybust into the water. The girls who were splattered screamed as if they were being drowned, and the boys laughed.

Doodle put the go-cart in the garage, thinking he would go out to the pool now and join in the fun there. But when he noticed Mr. Moreland pulling a bag of charcoal from a shelf, he asked, "Do you need help?"

Mr. Moreland smiled. "Since you've mentioned it, I could use a bit of assistance." He put the charcoal onto a wheelbarrow. "If you'll take this out for me, I'll bring the grill, and we'll soon be in business."

Next, Mrs. Moreland asked if Doodle wanted to help her bring out the refreshments. What he wanted to do was go swim with his classmates, but a few trips back and forth to the kitchen wouldn't take long. The last package was brought out, and Doodle was almost to the diving board when Mr. Moreland said it was time for everybody to come out of the pool.

Doodle was sorry not to have had a swim, but it didn't really matter. The go-cart was what was important. He thought about it while the hamburgers were being served and wondered if go-carts were so high-priced that only rich people like the Morelands owned them. He knew it wouldn't be polite to ask how much theirs had cost. Luke Stinson may have known it too —but it didn't keep him from asking.

"I don't remember the exact figure," said Mr. Moreland, not sounding as if he cared to talk about money. "Who's ready for another hamburger?"

Luke said, "Well, if you don't remember the *exact* price, do you remember *about* what it was?"

Mrs. Moreland laughed. Turning to her husband, she said, "Now, dear, it's no big secret. Anyone can find out the price by going into Helter's." Helter's was the main hardware store in Ripley. To Luke she said, "It cost two hundred dollars." Then she added, "And we're awfully glad you've enjoyed it this afternoon."

Doodle hoped he hadn't jumped when he'd heard the price. "Two hundred dollars!" he said to himself. "What a lot of money!" To him, anything over $25.50

was a lot of money. Even that was a big amount. The $25.00 was what he had saved from birthday and Christmas presents the year before. It was in his bank account in town. The 50 cents was spending money. He kept that in the cigar box in his dresser drawer.

After the hamburgers, sundaes were served. Mr. Moreland scooped up the ice cream, and the guests helped themselves to whatever toppings they liked best. Then it was time to go home.

Inez Proctor's father came for her and Doodle. They lived on neighboring farms, and Mr. Rounds, Doodle's father, had brought them to the party. It had been agreed that Mr. Proctor would pick them up afterwards. He was waiting, along with other parents, in the line of vehicles in front of the Moreland house.

It was almost sundown when Doodle got home, and he was glad the late afternoon chores had been done. His father had offered to do the milking for him, and his mother had said she would feed the chickens and gather the eggs. It was not often that he was invited to a party, and they'd do the work for him this time.

Before going into the house, Doodle looked out over his father's farm: outbuildings that seemed forever to need patching, fences in need of new posts, and beef cattle that had to be moved from one pasture to another for grazing. Beyond the open acres were woods, and deep in the woods were swampy low places and the Flint River.

Town and the Moreland estate were only nine miles away, Doodle knew. It only seemed that they were part of a different world.

Is
This Mule
Necessary?

One outbuilding was a big shed that had once been a wagon shelter. Mr. Rounds used part of it as a garage for his truck and tractor. The section that had once been a harness room was his workshop. There, on rainy days, he cleaned and repaired machinery. On sunny days, when repair jobs had to be done, he worked outside. A tree, a giant hickory, grew between the shed and the pasture fence, and he had built a long workbench in the shade of it. The bench faced the road and was high enough off the ground for a man to stand up and work.

Doodle liked helping his father when there were jobs to be done under the big tree. It was his favorite spot in the yard. He called the workbench his thinking bench, and whenever he didn't have anything else to do he sat

on the end of it and thought. Whenever Addie Flowers didn't have anything else to do, she came and stood by him. She would walk to the edge of the pasture and stretch her neck over the barbed wire till her head was almost in his lap. Then she would act as if she were helping him think. If he was not concerned about anything special, she might frisk about. But if he had something important on his mind, she seemed to know that serious thinking was required. At such times she seldom moved, not even to swat her tail at flies.

Addie Flowers was the only mule in the community. The other farmers used tractors for all their work. Mr. Rounds had been the first among them to buy a tractor, but he had kept Addie Flowers too. It did a man good, according to him, to hitch up a mule and plant a spring garden, or plow weeds out of a watermelon patch, or do any number of chores. He said it helped him stay "in tune with nature," making him feel closer to the earth from which he drew his living than he did when he was sitting high off the ground on the seat of a big machine.

The day after the party at the Morelands', Doodle helped his father sharpen the blades of the mower that was used in cutting hay. They were finishing the work when Mr. Franklin and Mr. Whit stopped at the edge of the road. Mr. Franklin called to Mr. Rounds, "Want to go across the river with us? The equipment at the

Nolan place is being auctioned off tomorrow, and we thought we'd have a look at it now."

"A good idea!" said Mr. Rounds. "Can you wait half a minute till I get the mower back under the shed?"

"Take your time," said Mr. Franklin, and the two men got out of the pickup truck and walked into the shade of the big hickory.

Seeing Addie Flowers at the edge of the pasture, her head over the fence as if she were supervising the work in the yard, Mr. Whit asked, "What sort of critter is that? I don't believe I've ever seen such an animal!" Mr. Rounds's friends were always teasing him about Addie. "Is this mule necessary?" they would ask, quoting from a tractor advertisement. Mr. Whit continued, "Don't you know the machine age has arrived?"

Mr. Rounds laughed. "It only got to right here!" With one foot he drew a mark like a boundary across the ground in front of him. "And me and Addie Flowers plan to hold the line."

"HOLD THAT LINE!" shouted Mr. Whit, as if he were cheering at a football game, and everyone laughed. "Yes, sir," he continued, "this place of yours is where old times meet the modern day. Eventually we might have to build a museum around this animal." He reached out to pat Addie, but she stepped back from him. "What did you say it is?" he asked Doodle. "A dinosaur or something?" Addie turned and walked away as if she objected to the comments that were being made.

Mr. Rounds spoke to Doodle. "Don't let him kid you. He hasn't been plowing with tractors all his life."

"Neither have I," said Mr. Franklin, "but I sure do admire them now!"

"Well," said Mr. Rounds. "I have to confess that I do too. Why, the amount of work one of them can do in a day just about breaks my back thinking about it. Even so, there's not enough money in the world to buy my last mule."

"Come nearer selling your wife or Doodle, wouldn't you?" asked Mr. Franklin.

"Couldn't get much for either one of them," said Mr. Whit, slapping Doodle on the back. "But mules ain't very high-priced either."

Addie Flowers was nearly to the stream at the end of the pasture when the men got into the truck and drove off. Doodle swung himself onto the thinking end of the big workbench, and Addie came back immediately.

"Well, hello, Duchess Addie!" said Doodle, and she turned and started away again. In a softer voice he called to her. "Come on, I was just teasing!" and she came back as if she understood. She stretched her neck over the fence and put her head almost in his lap. He patted her gently, then told her about Duchess Rose and the hand-tooled saddle, trimmed in turquoise, the Morelands had brought back from Mexico.

Next, he told her about the go-cart. Maybe it was because he sounded excited that she became excited too, stepping about gingerly. She acted as if she wanted to get started on something but wouldn't begin without Doodle.

Suddenly Doodle wanted to get started too. He hopped down from the bench and crawled between two strands of barbed wire into the pasture. "Come on," he said, "let's lay out a track for my go-cart." As if she had asked what he meant by "my go-cart," he explained, "The one I'll have someday."

The
Track

The pastures for the beef cattle were spread over the farm, but Addie's pasture was a small one. It covered three acres near the house. Addie shared it with Dainty, the milk cow—and Doodle and his friends whenever they got together for a ball game. It was smooth as a lawn, with a half dozen white oaks in the grassy area. Near the end there was a stream, and across the stream a thicket of sweet gum saplings.

Doodle walked about the pasture now as if he had never seen it. He had played there all his life, but not until today had he thought of it as a place to drive his go-cart—the one he would have someday. Addie followed as he walked up and down, circling one tree and going past the next one, sometimes turning around and going back in the direction from which he had come.

Every now and then he stopped and looked around
him.

At last he made up his mind: The track should be
oval shaped. It would run from the barn down one side
of the fence, almost reaching the stream before it would

22

curve across to the other side. "You can stand any-where in the middle," he told Addie Flowers, "and watch me drive around. And Dainty can watch too, or she can stay in the sweet gums." When Dainty wasn't busy eating grass, she usually rested among the saplings across the stream. She would chew her cud lazily, sel-dom taking any interest in Doodle—and none at all in Addie Flowers.

"Too bad Godfrey's not still around," Doodle told Addie. "He'd probably race me in the go-cart!" God-frey had been Dainty's calf, born a year ago, but he had been sold at the beginning of summer. He had been so playful that he would race Doodle from one end of the pasture to the other. Addie Flowers would stand off to the side and watch them running as if she had bet money on the race. It had been easy to guess which one she was backing. One afternoon Doodle had let God-frey win, and Addie had walked off in disgust.

Doodle had hated to see Godfrey sold, but he hadn't tried to talk his father into keeping the calf. Farm ani-mals were farm animals and not pets, no matter how gentle some of them became. They were still farm ani-mals when the time came to sell them—or to slaugh-ter them. Doodle had enjoyed playing with Godfrey, and now he enjoyed thinking about him. In his mind's eye he could see himself on a go-cart, racing around the oval-shaped track. Godfrey, his tail high in the air, would race after him, and Addie Flowers would stand by, watching.

Another idea came to him: Maybe instead of an oval he would lay out the track like a figure eight! On it, he could loop in and around and in again instead of going 'round and 'round. He walked the pasture in as perfect a figure eight as he could. It was no trouble to imagine himself speeding to the center of it, where the tracks would cross. If suddenly he turned off to the side he could imagine that Godfrey, who would be racing after him, wouldn't be able to slow down quickly enough to make the same turn. The calf would continue straight ahead. Doodle laughed when he thought of how puzzled Godfrey would look! But, of course, the calf had been sold. Still, it was fun to think about how it might have been.

Standing near the barn, he squinted his eyes, trying to see the pasture and to imagine the figure eight at the same time. He was picturing the track as clearly as if it were already there when his father returned home from his trip across the river with Mr. Franklin and Mr. Whit.

"On the way home," said Mr. Rounds, "we stopped near the bridge for me to show off my cornfield. And do you know that beavers have built dams just inside the swamp?"

"In the river?" Doodle asked.

"No," said his father. "In the stream that runs into it." He shook his head. "Something's got to be done about them. Those dams will eventually back water onto my bottomland."

"Dad," said Doodle, "do you know what go-carts are?"

"Yes, I do," said Mr. Rounds, "but I didn't know they were any help in getting rid of beavers."

"That's not what I meant," continued Doodle. "I just wondered if you'd ever seen a go-cart."

"I sure have," said Mr. Rounds. "They're interesting contraptions."

That was a good start, thought Doodle. He had been afraid his father would say, "They're dangerous, and don't you get any notion of wanting one!"

"Well, I was wondering what you might think of it if I had one of them."

"Why, I'd think highly of it, I suppose."

Doodle grinned. "Would you really?" he asked.

"I think they might be dangerous," said Mr. Rounds, and Doodle's grin disappeared. "That is, in the hands of someone too young to look after them, they'd be the wrong thing. But a boy like you might learn a good bit from one of them. You could learn about motors and what makes things run. Now that tractors carry the workload on farms, I wish I had a better mechanical background—especially when machinery breaks down." He kicked at a motor for a spraying machine that had been broken for a long time.

This was better than Doodle had hoped it would be. His father not only didn't consider go-carts foolish or dangerous, he considered them educational! Why, a go-cart was as good as his! "You mean you'll buy me one?"

His father looked at him. "Now, hold off! That's not what you asked me. Of course I won't buy you one. Do you have any idea what a go-cart costs?"

"Right at two hundred dollars," confessed Doodle. "At least some of them do."

"With all the other things that are needed around here," said Mr. Rounds, "your mother would skin us both if I spent that kind of money on a toy!"

Doodle knew it all right. His mother had thought Mr. Rounds was throwing away money when he bought Doodle two model airplane kits at one time. "But I'd learn something from it," he insisted. "You said so yourself." He also knew that one reason he and his father got along so well was because he didn't nag for things they couldn't afford, so he asked, "Then could I have a go-cart if I save enough money to buy it?" Mr. Rounds looked at him, but he hurried on, "You said a while ago, when I asked what you'd think of it if I had one, that—"

His father interrupted him. "Why, sure you can have one if you get up the price yourself. But it's dreaming, son, to think you can save that much money." He took off his hat and ran his handkerchief over his forehead. "But I guess we all need our dreams, don't we?" He smiled again, his eyes twinkling, and as he started away he asked Doodle, "What would you think of it if I rode into the yard one day in a bright blue Cadillac with white sidewall tires, red and black upholstering, and a horn that played 'You Are My Sunshine'?"

Doodle laughed, swinging himself onto the end of the workbench under the big tree. "I'd think highly of it!" he called to his father.

Mr. Rounds went into the house, and Doodle became serious. Almost immediately Addie Flowers appeared. She stood at the edge of the pasture and stretched her neck across the barbed wire. Doodle patted her. "Me and you've got some thinking to do," he said. "Some *real* thinking."

Doodle's Mule
Transportation:
One-way or Round-trip

"Why didn't I think of it before?" shouted Doodle, jumping down from the bench.

Addie Flowers, now that the thinking was done, swatted her tail at a horsefly while Doodle went over to the brooder house.

There had been a time when Mr. Rounds was a poultry farmer. Instead of the ten hens and a rooster the family kept now, he had raised chickens by the thousands. But prices got so low and feed so high that he switched to raising beef cattle. Chicken houses had been torn down, and lumber from them used in building shelters for the cattle.

A brooder house, where baby chicks were kept warm, had been built of concrete blocks, and it was still in the yard. Doodle used it as a place to store anything he believed might someday come in handy. "The treasure pile," his father called the collection of scraps. It included such things as boxes, old clothes, and bits of lumber. There were also pieces of metal and plastic in it that looked as if they had a purpose, whether or not anyone knew what the purpose was.

Doodle found a red crayon in the nail keg where he kept small items. Then he moved cardboard boxes until he came to the biggest one. With his pocket knife he cut out one side of the box and took it to the workbench. Addie watched as he printed on it: DOODLE'S MULE TRANSPORTATION: ONE-WAY OR ROUND-TRIP. At the bottom he put: ERRANDS ALSO. He had just finished the sign when his mother called that it was time to do the milking.

After he milked Dainty, it was time for supper, and during the meal the talk was about go-carts. Mrs. Rounds did not consider them very worthwhile, but she said that if Doodle could earn enough money to buy one, she supposed he could have it. Then they talked about the mule transportation business.

"It might just be a good idea," said Mrs. Rounds. "People are always wanting errands run."

"Will you need anything from the store tomorrow?" asked Doodle. "How would it be if I charged you a ten-cent 'carrying charge'?"

Mr. Rounds laughed, but Mrs. Rounds said sternly, "When I need anything from the store, young man, you'll bring it at no 'carrying charge.' " Then she smiled and added, "I've always wanted a fur coat, and I may start saving money to buy one. How would it be if I charged you a small fee for cooking your supper?"

Doodle laughed. "It would be undemocratic," he said—not knowing exactly what he meant. He'd heard his father say it when anything went against his idea of what was fair.

The next morning Doodle rode Addie out to look for customers. The sign was fastened onto one side of the burlap bag used as a saddle.

At the Mitchells', Gloria, who was a year younger than Doodle, was sitting in the swing on the front porch. She walked to the edge of the road to speak to him. When she heard about the money-making plan she told him it was a splendid idea. He felt encouraged; Gloria usually had money of her own, and maybe she'd want to ride Addie for the fun of it. "I wish there was some place I wanted to go," she said, "but I can't think of a single trip I really need to take." Maybe the reason Gloria usually had money was that she never spent any of it, thought Doodle. "But when you buy your go-cart, I'll look forward to having a ride in it," she said. Before he could answer, she added, "in the event you plan to offer rides to your friends—at no charge, of course."

The Proctors lived at the next farm. Inez was Doodle's age, and Buck was a year older. Neither of them was in the yard, but Inez came running out of the house when she saw Doodle. "What a good way to make money!" she said. Doodle would have been pleased, but Inez was always broke. "If I had a cent," she continued, "I would just think up some place to go on horseback, whether I needed to go there or not."

"It's a mule," said Doodle.

"Well, anyway, I'd sure help you out," said Inez. She was always big-hearted in talking about what she would do. Crossing her hands over her stomach, she said, "I cross my heart and hope to die if I'm not telling the whole, exact truth of just what I'd do—if I had any money." Because she would be so generous if only she were able, she said she was certain he would want her to be among the first to enjoy his go-cart—the one he was going to have someday. "You just let me know when to come over for a ride," she called as he left.

At the foot of the hill, Buck was shooting at tin cans on a ditch bank. He laughed at Doodle. "You'll never make enough money for a go-cart, no matter what you do. You're crazy to think you can."

"You'll be surprised!" said Doodle.

"Yeah, I'll be surprised all right!" snorted Buck. "And in the meantime if I wanted to go anywhere, I'd get there faster on my own two feet than on that moth-eaten critter you call a mule." That didn't bother Doodle; he was accustomed to Buck's smart-alecky comments. But Addie Flowers wasn't. Or maybe it was Buck's sharp voice that bothered her. Either way, she jerked impatiently on the reins. "Tell Inez she'll be welcome to ride my go-cart when I get it," said Doodle, as he and Addie were leaving. "But you needn't rush over."

Buck fired at a tin can, and the rifle shot scared Addie. It took no urging to get her to gallop all the way to the Bray's farm.

Doodle and Melvin Bray talked in the yard. "I wish you better luck with your plan than I had with mine," said Melvin. "Once I tried to sell rides on Dad's tractor, but I didn't make a penny. And Dad made me pay for the fuel I used—so I went broke in a hurry!"

"I don't have money to go broke with," said Doodle. He had decided the twenty-five dollars in his bank account was not to be spent on anything except a go-cart; neither was the fifty cents in the cigar box in his dresser. "But I do my part in keeping Addie in fuel," he said. "I help Dad haul hay and gather corn!"

After Doodle left Melvin's house, he met Katie Bates and her four-year-old twin brothers. They were going to the store at the junction of Highway 53 and the county road.

"We certainly would be interested in a ride," said Katie. "It's so hot I think I'll perish before we get to where we're going. Why, you were heaven sent!" She went on to say that all she had was a quarter, but if that was enough she would willingly pay it to Doodle if he would take her and the twins to the store, and home afterwards.

Doodle accepted the quarter and lifted the two boys onto the mule. Next, he held his hands for Katie to mount, and then he led Addie down the road. Doodle's Mule Transportation was doing cash business at last.

Just as Doodle stopped Addie in front of the store, Katie said she suddenly remembered something. "The reason we were coming to the store," she said, "was to spend that quarter I gave you. There was to be candy for the twins and a soda for me."

The twins started crying when she said there would be nothing. Doodle stood near Addie Flowers' head, looking at the ground. "Here," he said, "I'll give back a dime and you can still buy candy."

At that, the twins cried even louder, and Addie looked frightened. Her ears pricked up, and she had a wild look in her eyes that Doodle had never seen. She stepped about nervously, and he worried about what she might do. She never had run away from him, but he'd hate for her to start with his first passengers. The

twins would be thrown off and might break a leg or something, and Katie would be thrown off too, maybe cracking her head on a rock.

Quickly he gave back the quarter. The twins stopped crying at once and slid to the ground. Katie did not

wait for help either, but when she started into the store
she called back, "Now you wait and give us a ride
home! It was part of the bargain, remember?"

Doodle knew who had broken the bargain; but still,
if anyone was needing an errand run, he didn't know

who it might be. So he waited and gave Katie and the twins a ride back down the road. He was going that way, anyhow.

At home, he put Addie Flowers in her pasture. She went to the stream and had a drink, then she came to the fence. Doodle saw his father coming home from the fields and went to meet him, but Addie stayed near the bench. She stretched her neck across the barbed wire as if she would get on with some thinking for him.

A Profit
from the
Treasure Pile

"Are you quitting early?" Doodle asked his father. "The sun is still high."

"I started cutting the millet," said Mr. Rounds, "but changed my mind. It'll make better hay if I let it grow a bit longer. Anyway, I've got a job to do between now and night, and you can help me." Looking at a pile of small wooden posts, he said, "We'll need a few of those old bean stakes." Then he motioned toward the brooder house and asked, "Do you have any old clothes in your treasure pile?"

"Lots," said Doodle, "but I'm not sure any of them are your size."

Mr. Rounds laughed. "I want them for a scarecrow. But if you bring out anything better than what I'm wearing, I might swap!"

Doodle hurried to the brooder house. He had all

kinds of clothing there. Whenever he found anything along the roadside, even a shoe, he brought it home. He had wondered at times why anybody would throw away a shoe while riding, but maybe all the shoes hadn't been thrown from cars. Maybe somebody walking along had just stepped out of them because of aching feet. More often than not, it was one shoe he found instead of two, and that always puzzled him. He tried to make up a story to go with whatever he found.

He came to a big pair of overalls and thought of taking them for the scarecrow. The overalls were the ones he had found under the bridge down where Highway 53 crossed the Flint River. He believed they were the largest size made because they were far too big for anybody he knew. And they were not worn out. He couldn't imagine why anybody would throw away something that was almost new, and it had taken him a whole afternoon to make up a story about the overalls. He finally decided that the man who had worn them had gone into the river to cool off and somehow forgot to get dressed afterward. Doodle had asked several people if they had seen a big, fat man walking down the road naked, but nobody had. When he told his parents what he believed happened, Mr. Rounds thought it was funny, but Mrs. Rounds said that Doodle had a peculiar imagination.

"I thought it was better to imagine it the way I did,"

said Doodle, "than to think the man had drowned and floated down the river and out into the ocean where the sharks would eat him, bones and all." Mrs. Rounds had said yes, she guessed his first story was better.

Doodle put down the overalls, thinking of the fat man walking down the road without them, and picked up a pair of ragged pants. Then he found a frayed work jacket that was spattered with paint, a muddy baseball cap, and two shoes. The shoes didn't match each other, but a scarecrow wouldn't be fussy.

Mr. Rounds and Doodle sawed bean stakes and nailed them together for a frame. Then they put the clothes onto it. The baseball cap was nailed to a block of wood that was the head. They took the scarecrow to the back porch and tapped on the door. "What do you want?" called Mrs. Rounds.

"The Umpire wants a word with you!" answered Mr. Rounds, winking at Doodle.

Mrs. Rounds came onto the porch, and she laughed when she saw The Umpire. Then she went back into the house, and Doodle and his father took the scarecrow and fastened it to a stake in the watermelon patch. When they got back to the yard, a man stopped to ask the way to the river, and Doodle waited while his father gave directions. Often people got lost when they left the main highway in search of fishing spots along the Flint River.

After the man had gone, Mr. Ranking came. He stopped to chat, but he did not get out of his truck. Pointing toward the watermelon patch, he said, "I saw your scarecrow, and it reminded me that I've got to build one too. If I don't, the crows are going to eat all my cantaloupes."

"We'll make one for you," said Mr. Rounds. "Doodle and I are experienced scarecrow builders, so if you'll just step up to our tree-shaded workbench, we'll have one for you in no time!"

Mr. Ranking said he could build one at his house, but Mr. Rounds insisted that he and Doodle had the saw, hammer, and nails handy, and there were plenty of bean stakes and lots of old clothes. "Allow us to build a neighbor a scarecrow to be a neighbor to our scarecrow!" said Mr. Rounds. Mr. Ranking laughed as he got out of the truck and walked into the yard.

The second scarecrow had a different personality from the first. Its shirt was checkered with a long tail, and its pants were baggy. The head was made of hay, tied with binder twine and topped with a floppy hat.

"Do you think he'll scare the birds?" asked Mr. Ranking.

"He might fly away with them!" said Mr. Rounds, and everybody laughed.

As Mr. Ranking was leaving he thanked Doodle and his father, and he insisted that Doodle take fifty cents for the old clothes. "Buy yourself something you want," he said.

Doodle thanked him and put the fifty cents in his pocket. He knew that what he wanted was a go-cart. The money wouldn't buy it, but it was a start, and the day was ending with a profit after all.

He had started toward the house with his father when he noticed Addie Flowers. He had been so busy working on the scarecrows that he hadn't patted her once, although she had been at the end of the bench the whole time. He didn't go back and speak to her, but he did hold up the half-dollar for her to see.

The
Scarecrow
Business

Early the next morning Doodle worked under the giant hickory. Addie Flowers watched him saw bean stakes and nail them together, the way he and his father had done. All the farmers with melon patches, gardens, or late corn would be needing scarecrows, and he needed to earn money. The time was right for this very project.

A car stopped on the road, and two men asked the way to the river and the best fishing spots. "The river's down there," said Doodle, pointing in the direction of it. "But I don't know about the best spots. My father knows, if you'd care to stop and ask him. He's mowing the pasture this side of the bridge."

The river was narrow in places, wider in others, and there were pockets along its banks where the fishing was good. But they were hard to find.

The men drove away, and Doodle went to the brooder house and cut another piece from a cardboard box. With the crayon from the nail keg he lettered a sign: DOODLE'S SCARECROWS. Underneath he printed: BARGAINS. He put the sign on the end of the bench nearest the road and went back to work.

He put the big pair of overalls onto the biggest frame he had made. The overalls were so loose that he decided they should be stuffed with something. So he took the wheelbarrow and a rake and went to the pine grove beyond the house. He raked needles into a pile and then loaded them onto the wheelbarrow and pushed it to the workbench. The needles only half filled the overalls, and he had to haul another load to finish the job. Next, he added a white shirt and fastened the overalls straps over it. The shirt was ragged, but Doodle was certain it had once been somebody's Sunday best. He tied the French cuffs around wads of straw for hands. For a head he used a basketball that had come unstitched on one side. On top of the ball he put a straw hat, its brim turned up, and the scarecrow was finished. Doodle called it Mr. Jolly because it looked so happy. He imagined that the real man—the fat one who forgot to put his clothes on when he came out of the river— had looked very much like Mr. Jolly. Doodle was glad he hadn't drowned and floated out to the ocean.

The next scarecrow was average size—but little

compared to Mr. Jolly. It wore a pair of khaki pants and a leather jacket that was so moldy it was beginning to come apart. For a head Doodle stuffed leaves into an old sock, making a thin, pinched face.

"Are you playing dolls?" someone behind him asked. Doodle had been so busy he hadn't heard anyone walk into the yard, but once he heard that voice he didn't have to look to know that it belonged to Buck Proctor. Nobody else ever sounded as smart alecky.

Doodle looked around. "Does it look like I'm playing dolls?"

"Yes, it looks like you're playing dolls!" said Buck. "Wait'll I tell everybody."

"I'm making scarecrows," said Doodle. "I'm making them for sale."

"Oh, I get it!" said Buck. "It's one of your plans to make enough money for a go-cart." Then he laughed. "Like they say, all the fools ain't dead yet! I reckon you're proof of it." Finally he got around to saying his father had sent him over to borrow a wire stretcher. Doodle started to tell him that theirs was broken, but he knew his father and Mr. Proctor always lent each other tools. Anyway, the rest of the Proctor family couldn't help it that Buck was a smart aleck, so he found the stretcher, a tool for pulling barbed wire so that the strands would not droop while they were being nailed to fence posts.

44

"Well, I'd better start back," said Buck, "unless you'll drive me home in a go-cart!" On his way out of the yard he laughed as if there had never been a funnier joke.

Doodle went back to making the scarecrow, covering up most of its sock face with a felt hat that was dirty and greasy. To the part of the sock that showed, he fastened a scrap of tar paper. It was to have been a smile, but the ends went down instead of up, giving the face a mean look. Doodle called the scarecrow Mr. Sinister because it reminded him of a gunman called Sinister Slim in a television program. It looked so much like the gunman that he found an old toy pistol to put in one hand. Maybe birds would think the scarecrow would shoot them if they didn't get out of the field.

Just before lunch Doodle added prices to the bottom of his sign: "$1.00 and $1.50." He figured Mr. Jolly was worth more than Mr. Sinister. Being bigger, he should scare away more birds. Besides, the overalls were in such good condition they could be worn later if anybody cared for the idea and was fat enough.

Melvin Bray came in the afternoon to play ball, and he thought Doodle's project was a good one. "But charge more than a dollar for that little one," he said. "He looks so mean that he'd scare off lots of birds." Doodle admitted there was something funny about most scarecrows, but Mr. Sinister was downright

Doodle's
Scarecrow's
BARGAINS

frightening. He decided to charge $1.25 for the thin scarecrow and changed his sign to read "$1.00 *to* $1.50" instead of "$1.00 *and* $1.50." He'd make a dollar scarecrow later, but first he and Melvin wanted to practice their pitching in Addie's pasture.

They had just put on their gloves and started throwing the ball back and forth, Addie standing off to one side watching, when a car stopped. The man and woman in it were looking at the scarecrows, and Doodle hurried to the workbench. "Care to buy a scarecrow?" he asked.

"Thank you, no," said the man, and the woman added, "But they're the most interesting ones we ever did see!"

The man said, "We live in Atlanta and have a small garden. The birds get most of what we raise, but I guess we'd rather have the birds than the vegetables." Then he asked how to get to the best fishing spots along the river, and Doodle told them how to get to the river. "I can't tell you where the best spots are," he said, "because I don't know myself." Then he returned to the pasture and the game of pitch.

When Melvin went home, Doodle started another scarecrow. By late the next afternoon he had four. The third one reminded him of the one with the floppy hat that he and his father had made for Mr. Ranking. The fourth was like Mr. Jolly, except the overalls were rag-

47

ged and much smaller. All four were propped against the workbench, facing the road, and the sign by them made it clear that they were for sale.

Near sundown Mr. Rounds came home from the pasture where he had been mowing. He was in the yard with Doodle when Mrs. Rounds came out to see the scarecrows. "Why, they're works of art!" she told Doodle. "Maybe you'll grow up to be a sculptor!"

His father said, "If anybody hereabouts needs help in scaring crows they'd better purchase themselves a Doodle-made scarecrow!" He and Mrs. Rounds started inside, and when Doodle didn't go with them, his mother called, "It's time for supper!"

"I'll be there as soon as I put my scarecrows inside the shed for the night."

"Inside the shed?" asked his father.

"They might get rained on," explained Doodle. "I want to keep them looking new." His parents laughed, and Addie Flowers, who had been standing at the fence, turned away as if she were hiding a smile. Doodle supposed it did sound funny to say he wanted to keep scarecrows looking new, so he laughed with them.

The Flint River

Every day Doodle put the scarecrows and the sign in front of the workbench, and at sundown he put them away. People stopped, mostly to ask directions. Nobody wanted to buy a scarecrow.

At the end of a week he went out to look for customers. He tied the rope to Addie Flowers' halter, threw the burlap bag across her back, and started down the road. Maybe he could find somebody who wanted to buy a fat scarecrow, a skinny one, or one in between.

"No," said Mr. Mitchell, Gloria's father, "I don't need a scarecrow since I didn't plant any watermelons this year." Then he added, "But we'd be pleased to have a melon or two from your dad's patch when they get ripe—if you're planning to neighbor any of them out." By neighbor them out, he meant give them away. Doodle could see where Gloria came by her habit of not spending any money.

Mr. Davis, at the next farm, said, "Yes, I have a watermelon patch, but the birds haven't discovered it yet, so there's no problem. Thank you just the same."

And Mr. Whit said, "Why, the birds are going to eat every one of my melons, and they're after my grapes too, but instead of scarecrows I plan to put up long strings with rags tied to them. It's more scientific."

At the Proctors', Buck was helping his father repair a fertilizer spreader out near the tractor shelter. Doodle tied Addie to a post and went to talk with them. He explained to Mr. Proctor, "I've got me a project, making and selling scarecrows. By chance, would you care to buy one?"

Mr. Proctor smiled. "I guess not, thanks. I made one last week to stand guard over the cantaloupes, and that's all I've got that birds ever bother."

Buck laughed. Turning to Doodle he said, "You're getting rich, I see! Maybe you'll buy two or three go-carts instead of just one!" He laughed until Mr. Proctor told him it was not all that funny.

On the way out the driveway, Doodle waved at Inez. She was standing in a window of the Proctors' house.

At other farms there were other reasons a scarecrow

was not wanted. Finally Doodle went home. He took the last two scarecrows he had made and put them in the cornfield with The Umpire. If one scarecrow was helpful, maybe three would do an even better job. He stored Mr. Jolly and Mr. Sinister in the brooder house. Mr. Sinister looked so scary that Doodle turned him to the wall, and the brooder house looked brighter with only Mr. Jolly keeping watch over the scrap pile.

Doodle went back to the workbench and swung himself onto it. Looking out over Addie's pasture, he could see himself riding around it in his go-cart—the one he would have someday. He pictured himself on an oval track first, then he pictured one shaped like a figure eight. He reminded himself that he would never be riding there on any kind of track if he didn't get busy. So he stopped dreaming about how grand it was going to be to own a go-cart and tried to think of a way to earn money to buy one.

Addie Flowers, who had been resting in the shade of one of the water oaks, came to the edge of the fence and stretched her neck across the barbed wire. As if she had whispered something to him, Doodle sprang from the bench. "This time we've got it for sure!" he said.

In the brooder house he cut a long piece of cardboard from a box that probably had once held an ironing board. On it he printed with the big crayon:

DOODLE AND COMPANY, FISHING GUIDES. He showed it to Addie Flowers. "You're the 'and Company'," he told her.

At supper he asked his father, "What would you say if I decided to be a fishing guide?"

"I didn't know you knew your way up and down the river well enough to set yourself up as a guide," said Mr. Rounds.

"I could learn," said Doodle.

"In that case, I'd say it's a good idea," said his father. Doodle didn't tell him that he planned to learn and guide at the same time. But maybe it wouldn't be right to charge anybody till he knew more about the river. He and Melvin Bray and some of their friends had played along the banks of the Flint River, mostly down near the bridge where they swam. At another spot they played on vines that grew along the bank, swinging out over the water and daring each other to drop into it. But he had never really explored the swamp or tried to find the hidden, deep places where large fish could be caught.

Next day, he and Addie headed toward the river, cutting across the far pasture where his father's cattle were grazing. Half a dozen of the cows looked up and then went back to grazing, but the bull, Robinson, lifted his head and kept an eye on Doodle and Addie.

Robinson was gentle, not mean the way some bulls

were, but he didn't have much personality—not like Godfrey. Doodle wished Godfrey had been born a purebred Angus; maybe then his father would have raised him for a stock bull. Or maybe he wouldn't have.

Mr. Rounds bought a young bull every few years to introduce new blood lines to the herd. If Godfrey had been an Angus, he still might have been sold, but he would have been bought by someone wanting to introduce a new line to a different herd. He would have grown up to be a stock bull like Robinson. But Godfrey had been a scrub Jersey, and Doodle knew what became of scrub Jersey bulls. His father had once said, "They have a one-way ticket to the slaughterhouse."

On the trail that led from the pasture into the woods, Addie had gone less than ten feet when she stopped. "Come on!" coaxed Doodle, but Addie eased backward. "Now what's the matter?" asked Doodle, just as he saw that a giant highland moccasin snake was curled up on the path ahead. He hopped down and quickly found a long stick. With one whack he killed the snake. He'd had practice killing snakes, which should be one thing that would recommend him as a guide. Then he and Addie Flowers went on their way. Big patches of wild strawberry vines grew near the trail, and he told Addie, "Let's remember these till next spring and come pick us some berries when they get ripe!" Soon the trail became so overgrown with weeds that Doodle had

trouble staying on it, but finally he came out at the river.

All afternoon he searched out old trails and paths, riding Addie when the growth was not too dense. Toward twilight he left the woods, being careful to watch for snakes when he came to the spot where he had killed the moccasin.

In the pasture Robinson and the cows were lying on a hillside, settled down for the night, and by the time Doodle arrived home it was dark. He milked Dainty by lantern light.

Mrs. Rounds made Doodle promise to come home earlier in the future. She had been persuaded by him and his father—against her better judgment, she insisted—that he could explore the woods and swamp. But she had no intention of letting him stay on the river after dark, just him and Addie Flowers. She shook her finger at Mr. Rounds and Doodle. "There are times when you have your way, and there are times when I have mine. And this is one of them!"

The next day Doodle took a bush blade to the swamp and cut out undergrowth along the trails where it was thickest. Some of the trails were so overgrown that he doubted anyone had been along them since Indian times. It gave him a good feeling to cut through dense growth and come into a clearing. He could imagine how pioneers felt in reaching new lands. He could also see why it took them a long time to get to where they were going. Progress was so slow that he worked for two weeks before he was satisfied that he could lead fishermen along paths that would be easy to follow.

"You've done a powerful good job of it!" said Mr. Rounds, surprised at how clear the paths were. He and Doodle had gone fishing on Saturday after lunch.

During the afternoon Mr. Rounds caught a large bass and an even bigger pike. "Bring your customers to this spot," he said, pulling another bass from the water. The only fish Doodle caught was a perch, and it was not big enough to take home for supper. He threw it back into the river to grow.

On Monday he fished by himself, trying different spots along the river. He caught an eel that slipped off the hook, two bluegill that were so tiny he threw them back, and an old shoe with the toe cut out. Earlier he might have carried the shoe home to his scrap collection, but there were other things he wanted to think about now.

School was not one of them, but it started the following week anyway. He was in the sixth grade, and some of his friends from last year were in his homeroom, and some were not. But he could see all of them on the playground—all except his cousin, Glenn Carter. Glenn's parents, Aunt Peggy and Uncle Roy, were sending him to a private school in Atlanta. He rode back and forth in a station wagon driven by one of the older students.

Doodle rode a bus, leaving home early in the morning and not getting back till after four o'clock, but the days were still long. There was time to be a guide during part of the afternoon.

Every day he sat on the workbench when he got home, his sign in front of him, but nobody came along —except Melvin Bray to play pitch and Buck Proctor. "Fishing guides make lots of money!" Buck called one day when he rode past on his bicycle. Another time he yelled, "Still having lots of customers, I see!" Both times he laughed till he was out of hearing distance. Doodle worried that nobody else came along.

"To a lot of people summer's over," explained Mr. Rounds.

"Why?" asked Doodle. "The weather's still hot."

"I know, but once Labor Day has come and gone and schools are back in session, folks figure summer's over. In the country we go by nature instead of the calendar. I can't start my fall plowing till it rains enough to soften the earth, no matter if the first Monday in September is already behind us."

"But fish will be biting," said Doodle. "They don't know about the first Monday in September either."

"Yes," agreed his father, "and a few fishermen will

be coming this way on Saturdays for a while yet. But I'm afraid I'll be keeping you busy."

"On Saturdays?" asked Doodle.

"We'll have to clean and oil equipment that won't be needed till next spring," answered his father, "and we must walk all the fences." By walk the fences, he meant that he and Doodle would go along every fence of every pasture, making repairs. "And you can help me build shelters for the salt blocks. The blocks last longer if they're protected." He mentioned other tasks to be done before cold weather, and for weeks afterwards Doodle helped with them. It was not until the end of October, the very last day of it, that there was a Saturday with no special work to be done. Doodle sat out by the road all day, his fishing guide sign in front of him, but nobody came along. He guessed he'd learned his way through the swamp and along the river for nothing.

As he sat he wondered if he would ever have a go-cart. For the first time he couldn't see in his mind's eye a clear picture of one of them racing across Addie's pasture. He wondered if he'd ever get to ride a go-cart again, even one belonging to someone else.

Elsie Moreland was not in his homeroom this year, so he was missing the Halloween party the Morelands were giving for her classmates. It was being held while he was thinking about it. The weather was too cold for swimming, and the go-cart and Duchess Rose were probably providing the entertainment. But Elsie's brother Donald was at home now, and maybe he wouldn't want her guests playing with his go-cart. Maybe he wouldn't be as generous with it as Mr. Moreland had been. That made Doodle feel better. Then he realized this was selfish—which made him feel worse. Anyway, he didn't wish it; he didn't wish the other boys weren't having fun just because he couldn't be with them. He hoped the party was just like the one on the Fourth of July and that all the boys, and any of the girls who cared about it, were getting to ride as often as they pleased. Remembering the day he had first seen a go-cart made him feel good again.

The
Good
Things
———————

On the second day of November Mr. Rounds sold Dainty. It was not a big surprise to anyone. Mrs. Rounds had said for a long time that it would be easier —and maybe cheaper—to buy milk and butter than to keep a milk cow.

Mr. Maxwell, who lived across the river, backed his truck up to the loading chute, and he and Mr. Rounds stood in the yard, talking. Doodle watched his father put seventy-five dollars, the price of Dainty, into his pocket.

"I'm proud to have a milk cow," said Mr. Maxwell, adding that he had been brought up on a farm but had lived in Atlanta thirty years. Recently he had moved back to the country because of his children. "I want them to see that milk and eggs come from cows and chickens instead of supermarkets," he said.

"It's too bad," said Mr. Rounds, shaking his head, "but I'm afraid the day will come when only a handful of people will know how to raise the food for all of us."

"Yes," agreed Mr. Maxwell, leaning against the thinking end of the workbench. "My kids were beginning to believe that vegetables grow in tin cans on grocery shelves." He reached his hand out toward Addie Flowers. Addie, who usually didn't come to the bench to visit with anyone except Doodle, stretched her neck over the barbed wire. She let Mr. Maxwell pat her as if they were old friends.

"I don't know what the country's coming to!" said Mr. Rounds, and the two men went on talking about the differences between city and farm life, and the old days and nowadays.

Doodle took a rope to the sweet gum thicket at the end of the pasture and brought Dainty back to the yard. She balked when he tried to lead her up the platform of the loading chute, and his father and Mr. Maxwell got behind her and pushed.

"She didn't want to go riding," said Mr. Rounds when she had been loaded onto the truck, "but we talked her into it!"

Doodle was glad there would be no more milking chores. At the same time, it was a bit sad to see Dainty being hauled away. He never had liked her a lot, but still, she had always been there, and he had milked her twice a day. Also, Godfrey had been her calf.

During supper Doodle and his mother talked about how they'd miss Dainty and how there would be less work now that she was gone. "I'll throw away the strainer and the buckets and the churn and everything else!" said Mrs. Rounds.

Mr. Rounds laughed. "Well, if you can be that extravagant, I guess I can give away the money I got for Dainty."

"You'll do nothing of the sort!" said Mrs. Rounds.

"I will if I please!" said Mr. Rounds, and Doodle laughed. He liked it when his parents had arguments when neither was really mad. Mr. Rounds said that the money was needed on the farm, wasn't it always, but for a change nothing was *urgently* needed. He said it would be a splendid idea to give away what he called "the Dainty cash." Faking anger, he told Mrs. Rounds, "And you don't know but what you're the very one I was planning to give it to!"

"In that case, you have my permission. Just hand it over!" She held out her hand.

"Very well," said Mr. Rounds, "here you are: twenty-five dollars!"

Mr. Rounds turned to Doodle. "And here's twenty-five dollars for you." Looking at what was left, he added, "And that leaves twenty-five for me to spend as I please!"

Doodle thanked his father for the twenty-five dollars. He thanked him again and counted the money over and over. It had a good feel to it.

Mr. Rounds teased Mrs. Rounds and Doodle. He reminded them that during supper they had talked about how much they would miss Dainty, in spite of the

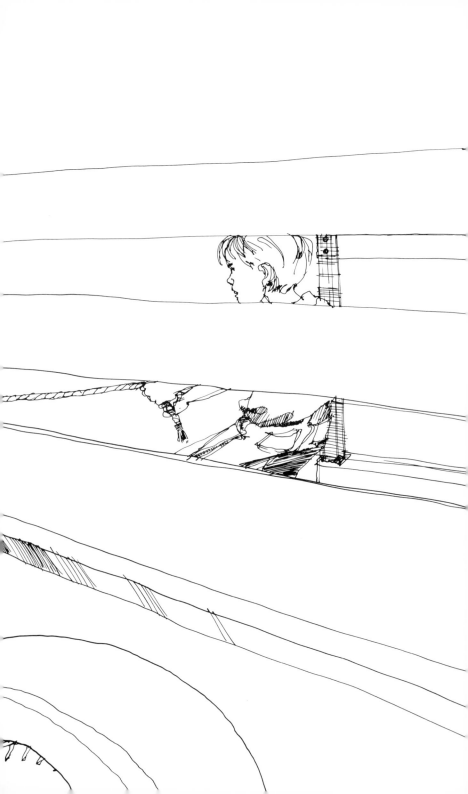

work they'd be saved. "But after I shared the money with you I haven't heard one tiny peep about anyone missing a cow!" He pretended to be ashamed of them. "Why, money is filthy!" he added, throwing his wallet across the room into a trash can. Then he raced Doodle to get it back. All of them were laughing at bedtime about their feelings toward money: They sometimes thought it was the cause of trouble, then first thing they knew they'd be especially happy about getting their hands on some of it! "It's possible to spend money on things that are worthwhile," said Mr. Rounds, as if someone had said it wasn't. Doodle knew exactly what he wanted that was worthwhile.

Mr. Rounds continued, "Of course, I may spend part of mine for pure fun!" And on Saturday night he took the family into town to the carnival. It was a small one on its way to Florida for the winter. "They don't even have a cotton candy machine!" complained Mr. Rounds. A joke he had once told on himself had to do with his going to a carnival when he was a boy. He had spent all his money on cotton candy.

"Let's treat Doodle to a few rides," said Mrs. Rounds, and Mr. Rounds agreed: "Good idea!"

Doodle asked, "Could I have the money they'd cost instead of taking the rides?"

Mr. Rounds laughed. "I suppose you could."

"I suppose you *could not!*" said Mrs. Rounds. "Go-

66

cart or no go-cart, you're not going to start bargaining for money at every turn!'"

In a way Doodle was glad his mother objected. He had always liked rides at a carnival, and he enjoyed them at this one, especially the bump cars. But even they were not as exciting to him as a ride in a go-cart would have been.

Sunday afternoon Doodle helped his father drive the cattle into a big pen in the pasture nearest the river. There they separated the steers from the rest of the herd. They were to be taken to a cattle auction.

"Can't I just skip school tomorrow and go to the auction too?" Doodle asked at bedtime.

Mrs. Rounds said, "You know what the answer to that will be!" When Doodle didn't say anything, she asked, "Now don't you?"

"I guess I do," he said, and the next morning he went to school as usual.

It was late afternoon when Mr. Rounds returned home. "Our steers weighed out heavier than I'd thought they would," he said, "and prices were high. You can't beat that for a combination: a bumper crop and bumper prices." It was the combination that gave him what he called "a substantial profit." "I think I'll throw some of it away!" he said, giving two ten-dollar bills to Doodle.

His father didn't really consider the money thrown away, Doodle knew, because Mr. Rounds was anxious for him to have a go-cart. As if he had to give a reason for being so generous, he explained: "You don't have an allowance the way some young people do. But you help with the work around here, so it's only fair to give you a bit of the profits." Doodle could tell from the way he said it that he was arguing with Mrs. Rounds before she could say, "You're spoiling Doodle." She didn't say it, so he guessed his father won the argument.

Other times when Mr. Rounds had sold cattle, he had given Doodle a few dollars—but never twenty! The money, along with his twenty-five dollars from the sale of Dainty, would go into the bank, and his account would total seventy dollars! He began thinking again about the track he would lay out in Addie's pasture for his go-cart—the one he would have someday—even though he needed almost a hundred and thirty dollars more.

There weren't many ways for him to try to earn money in late fall and winter. If he lived in town, chances of finding a job would be better. There he might have a paper route, or wash automobiles, or do odd jobs in stores. But what could he do in the country? Surely there was something, if only he could think of it. But first he had to think about tomorrow's homework, and he suddenly remembered he had left his arithmetic book at school. He hopped up and ran outside. It was nearly sundown, and he would have to hurry.

Addie Flowers was at the pasture gate, so he tied a rope to her halter, threw the burlap bag over her back, and rode over to see if Alice Elton would let him copy the problems from her book.

Alice had already done her homework, and she lent the arithmetic book to Doodle. As he was leaving, he stopped to speak to her brother Jess, who was in the tool shed putting traps together. "I plan to try my luck at trapping this winter," he told Doodle.

"Will you have time to do all the skinning and stuff that trappers have to do," asked Doodle, "and go to school too?" Jess was in the tenth grade, and Doodle had heard that in high school there was even more homework than sixth graders were assigned. Also, Jess was a star basketball player—the only sophomore on the varsity.

"I won't have to do any of the skinning," said Jess. "Dad knows a man from the other side of Stockbridge who's a country fur dealer."

"What does that mean?" asked Doodle.

"It means he has a regular route," said Jess. "And he'll come along every few days during cold weather to check with anybody who wants to sell animals to him. Why don't you do some trapping too? There's big

money in it, and you've got good places along the river on your dad's farm."

"Won't you be going up and down the river?"

"I'll be farther down it than you," said Jess. He pointed in the opposite direction. "And we have three springs where I'll put some of my traps."

Doodle thanked him for the suggestion and left. On the way home he remembered the beavers that were building dams. Wasn't water in their ponds damaging his father's cropland? He could trap the beavers and be doing his father a favor at the same time. It was a way to earn money at last, and he was thinking about it when he came to the Proctors' house. Almost past it, he heard the shrill voice he could recognize anywhere. Buck was leaning over the railing of a side porch. "Hey, Doodle," he yelled, "have you bought yourself a go-cart lately?" He laughed as if it were the funniest joke in the world.

"Not yet," answered Doodle, pretending he thought Buck was being friendly. "But I expect to buy one soon."

The
Traps

"What would you think if I decided to trap those beavers that are about to drive you off your own land?" asked Doodle.

Mr. Rounds put down the copy of *Newsweek* he had been reading. "I'd think you were a noble son, wanting to help your poor ol' father solve his beaver problem. At the same time, I'd think you had in mind a way of earning money for a go-cart!" Doodle grinned, and his father added, "But those beavers must go, there's no doubt about it!"

Mrs. Rounds asked, "Couldn't you destroy their dams? Wouldn't that get rid of them?"

"It would discourage them," said Mr. Rounds. "And if I hauled off all the limbs and sticks so they couldn't use them again, and if I cut down the trees nearby, they'd find it hard to build back in the same places.

Chances are they'd move upstream, and I'd solve the problem by passing it along to my neighbors."

"You can't do that," agreed Mrs. Rounds. "But still, it's cruel to trap them."

"Maybe it is," said Mr. Rounds. "It's also cruel to shoot them, but I'm going to get rid of them one way or another." He looked at Doodle and winked. "Your mother talks out of both sides of her mouth! Out of one side she says it's inhumane to trap animals, and out of the other side she says she would feel warm and awfully dressed up in a fur coat!"

Doodle expected his mother to argue, but she said, "Yes, I know. I may decide I don't want a fur coat."

"And I was all set to buy one for you!" teased Mr. Rounds. Then he said seriously, "I wouldn't want Doodle trapping anything that's not bothering anyone or that's in danger of becoming extinct. But beavers are not on the verge of that, around here, and they're causing us real hardship."

"Oh, all right!" said Mrs. Rounds, and Doodle brought out the catalog Jess Elton had lent him. He and his father got busy, deciding first on the number of traps needed and their sizes. "And you'll need rubber boots," said Mr. Rounds, "and a pair of shoulder gauntlets."

"What are shoulder gauntlets?" asked Doodle.

"Long gloves," explained Mr. Rounds, flipping

through the catalog. "Yes, here they are." He pointed to a picture. "With this pair you can reach under water and still keep your hands dry. In freezing weather you'll be glad you've got 'em."

Doodle took the catalog and read about the gauntlets. Then he looked at the pictures and write-ups of other supplies. "Will I need steel wire and slide clips?"

"I have wire you can use," said Mr. Rounds, "and I can make slide clips for you out of scraps of metal. No need to buy everything new."

When the order was made out, Mr. Rounds said, "It's going to cost you thirty-eight dollars, plus tax and shipping charges."

"*That* much?" said Doodle. "Are you sure you added it right?"

His father laughed. "You'd better check me on it," he said, and Doodle went over the figures.

"You're right. But I sure hate to spend thirty-eight dollars."

"Plus tax and shipping charges," said Mr. Rounds. "But it's the way of business! Lack of cash has kept many a good man from making a fortune. Of course, if you don't think enough of your venture to back it with part of your savings, you'd just as well—"

Doodle interrupted him. "Oh, I think enough of it. Would you mind drawing the money out of the bank for me when you go to town?"

"I'll advance it to you," said his father, "so you can get the order off tomorrow. But remember that it's a loan, not a gift, this time. You must pay me back when you sell all the beavers you'll trap."

"And what if he doesn't trap any?" asked Mrs. Rounds.

"Then he can draw money from the bank and pay his debt," said Mr. Rounds, starting to figure shipping charges. He used a postal chart on the back page of the catalog.

The order was mailed before breakfast, and in the weeks ahead Doodle waited. He had never known a mail order to take such a long time in being filled. Thanksgiving arrived before the traps did. He wished he could have spent the holiday trapping, but instead he spent his spare time reading a book Jess Elton had lent him. It was one Jess had checked out of the high school library. Doodle had already read the books on trapping that were in the library of the elementary school and the ones in the bookmobile from the public library.

Late Monday afternoon Jess brought the country fur dealer, the man his father knew from the other side of Stockbridge, and introduced him to Doodle and Mr. Rounds. When the man learned that Doodle planned to catch beavers only, he asked, "Don't you want to set some traps for minks and otters?"

Doodle wanted to say, "Yes, sure I do! I want a go-cart so much I'll do anything to get one!" But he looked at his father and then back at the fur dealer. "No, sir," he said. "Minks and otters are not bothering us."

"What about muskrats?" said the man. "You'll catch some of them in the same traps you set for beavers."

Mr. Rounds said, "That's okay. They're something of a pest."

The country fur dealer explained that he would buy the muskrats. "But the beavers are the main thing," he said. "And I'll pay for them according to size." Then he handed Doodle a small can. "Here's some lure I mixed up that you can have," he said. "Some people say you don't need it if your traps are in the right place, but a little of it won't hurt."

Doodle opened the can and sniffed, immediately drawing back his head and making a face. The man laughed. "I know what you mean!" he said. "But beavers think it's great!"

Mr. Rounds asked, "How'd you make it?"

"I ground up a scent gland and mixed it with a little sawdust and mineral oil. It's the castor that makes it smelly." Doodle knew that castor was a substance from certain glands of the beaver.

After the man left, Doodle had a good time thinking

about all the money he was going to make. He wished there was something he could do to get his traps in a hurry, but he had to wait all the next week for them. It was not until Saturday that they arrived.

He opened the package and checked the traps. Then he put on the boots and gauntlets and wore them into the kitchen where his mother was washing breakfast dishes. "You look like someone from another planet!" said Mrs. Rounds. "Is your spaceship in the yard or on the roof?"

Doodle laughed with her and then took his traps outside. He called Addie Flowers, and she came and stood patiently while he packed his trapper's supplies into a big canvas bag, which he put across her back. Then he mounted and was riding out of the yard when his father came along. "If you'll wait till after lunch," said Mr. Rounds, "I'll go with you."

"I'll wait," said Doodle, climbing to the ground. He took the bag off Addie's back and turned her into the pasture again. "Don't worry," he told her, patting her rump, "we'll go this afternoon."

As soon as lunch was finished, Mr. Rounds and Doodle headed toward the beaver pond. Addie followed them, the canvas bag containing the trapping gear across her back.

In the bottomland where the cornfield had been

flooded, they came to the edge of the water. "Let's set some traps on this side," said Doodle. "Then we can go around to where water's backed into the swamp."

"All right," said Mr. Rounds, "and if you were a beaver, where would you go into the water?" He and Doodle looked around, and both of them pointed at a sloping bank near an old stump. "Right there!" they said at the same time, agreeing that a trap should be placed near it.

First Doodle fastened one end of a long piece of wire to a large rock, which he dropped into the water. He threaded the free end of the wire through the slide clip his father had made for him and staked the end of the wire to the bank. "Done like an expert!" said Mr. Rounds, who had sat on the stump while Doodle put the slide wire in place. "Now set the trap!"

Doodle set it in shallow water, covering it with a few water-soaked leaves. Then he fastened the short chain on it to the slide clip and tested to see that it could only be pulled in the direction of the big rock and not toward the bank. "Somehow it doesn't seem right," he told his father, "to rig it so a beaver can only pull into deep water and drown."

"It would be even more cruel not to rig it that way," said Mr. Rounds. "Then anything that was caught would be held captive and couldn't get away."

"I don't want it to get away!" said Doodle.

"Yes, but what if it were attacked by a natural enemy and couldn't fight back or escape? It would suffer in any event. Beavers have been known to gnaw off their own legs in order to free themselves. So the drowning method, strange as it seems, is more humane than not rigging the trap with a slide clip."

Doodle took a double handful of wet soil and patted it into a mound on the bank. Then he opened the can of lure and sprinkled a bit of it on top.

"Very good!" said his father. "It looks like a mud-dob scent station a beaver might have made."

"It smells like one too!" said Doodle.

Three more traps were used on the open side of the pond, and another was set near a beech tree. By then they were getting into the swamp. "Instead of tying the ends of your slide wires to stakes," said Mr. Rounds, "you can just tie them to the base of small saplings or bushes."

Doodle put one trap in the water's edge by a rotted log and another near a big rock. He put others at locations a beaver might use for sliding into the pond or climbing out of it. He took a careful look around each time so he wouldn't have trouble finding the spots again.

When they returned home, Mr. Rounds helped Doodle mount a big wire basket onto an old horse blanket that was in the scrap collection in the brooder house.

The blanket could be put across Addie's back with a couple of leather straps to hold it in place. "Just the thing," said Doodle, "for bringing home all the beavers and muskrats I'll catch!"

At supper he and his father told Mrs. Rounds about the places the traps had been set. Mr. Rounds said, "Doodle knows more about the swamp than I do. All the exploring he did for his guide service is coming in handy."

"Just proves that anything we learn is never wasted," said Mrs. Rounds, and Doodle and his father continued to talk about what they called the choice locations they had found for the traps. They tried to guess which ones would turn out best, and his father talked so excitedly that Mrs. Rounds said, "I didn't know you were going to give up farming to become a trapper, too!"

All of them laughed. "I went today," said Mr. Rounds, "but after this, Doodle is on his own."

But the next morning when Doodle got up at dawn to go check the traps, Mr. Rounds got up too. "I'd like to be in on the fun this first time," he said.

Addie Flowers was waiting at the pasture gate as if she had an appointment with them, and soon the wire basket was on her back. Doodle could have ridden in front of it, but he walked with his father, leading Addie. They shivered as they cut across the far pasture. Although the weather was mild for December, it was chilly at such an early hour, and the dampness near the river made it seem still colder. "Wouldn't it be great," said Mr. Rounds, "if you've had beginner's luck and caught something in every trap?"

The Risky Business

The traps on the open side of the pond had not been disturbed. The ones in the swamp were empty too.

On the way home Mr. Rounds said, "Trapping's not supposed to be extra good till cold weather, so don't be discouraged."

"I'm not," said Doodle. "One of the books I read called trapping a risky business. It said that some people who start out to be trappers don't have a knack for it and never catch anything."

"Oh, I think you'll have a knack for it," said Mr. Rounds.

That night Doodle set his alarm clock, and when it sounded in the morning he got up. His mother came into his room a few minutes later. "I heard your alarm," she said. "But you mustn't go into the swamp while it's still dark."

"I'm not planning to go into the swamp till after school," he said. "But can't I take the lantern and ride Addie over to the open side of the pond? It'll be daylight by the time we get there, and I'll check the traps outside the swamp and be back in a little while."

Mrs. Rounds said that no, he could not, but it began to get lighter while they were talking. Finally she said it was all right for him to be on his way.

There was not anything in the traps, and at breakfast he looked so disappointed that Mr. Rounds said, "I thought you were *not* going to be discouraged!"

Doodle grinned. "I'm not," he said, hopping up from the table. He grabbed his books and ran out to catch the bus to school.

When he got home in the afternoon, he and Addie Flowers went to the swamp, but nothing had been caught in the traps there.

After supper he started to turn on television, but stopped when his mother said, "Don't forget your lessons! They're not to be neglected!"

"Yes, ma'am, I know," said Doodle. He was supposed to finish his homework each night before he watched even one program on television. Sometimes when a favorite program was scheduled he would skip over part of the work, pretending he had done a better job of it than he had.

Mrs. Rounds sat down to read the newspaper. "We'll have an understanding," she said. "If you find it's not possible to do your trapping and keep up your school load, the trapping is over." She snapped her fingers to show how quickly it would come to an end.

Doodle got out his books and began to study. If a poor report card would finish his trapping, that was one risk he could avoid.

After a few days his new schedule was set: He checked some of his traps in the mornings, the rest in the afternoons when he got home from school. The sun rose late and set early, and there wasn't enough light at either end of the day to do everything. At night he studied.

He wouldn't have minded the studying or missing his favorite programs on television, or checking traps at dawn and again toward sundown—if only he could catch something. There were times when he thought trapping was too much trouble. Then he would think about his go-cart, the one he would have someday, and know that it was worth any amount of trouble.

Jess Elton wasn't having any luck either. "Cold weather's all we need!" he told Doodle on the school bus one morning.

The weather continued mild, and another morning Jess said, "What if this turns out to be one of those winters when we don't have any freezes to speak of?"

Buck Proctor, across the aisle, said, "Then we won't speak of them!" He laughed as if he had never heard anything funnier.

That very night it turned cold.

Doodle wished he had worn a heavier jacket as he and Addie started out to make the rounds of the traps. But he didn't mind being cold; wasn't freezing weather what he had been wanting? Trapping was sure to be good now. He wouldn't be surprised to find a beaver in every trap.

The first one was empty, but he knew there would be beavers in the rest of them. Probably there would be more than he could get in the wire basket; he would have to make two trips. But all of the traps were empty.

Next morning he told himself that he wouldn't be greedy and want a beaver in every trap; he would settle for an equal number of beavers and muskrats.

Again the traps were empty, and on the third day of the cold spell, as he made his way across the pasture at dawn, ice spewing up along the trail, he knew he would settle for just one muskrat. But still nothing had been caught.

He doubted there were any muskrats or beavers left in the county. Maybe they had all moved away or something. "No," said Jess Elton. "I've had some luck at last. I caught two muskrats this morning."

School let out early that afternoon because of a teachers' meeting, and when Doodle got home he hurried to the swamp. Nothing had been caught, and he tested the traps to make certain they were working. He also added fresh lure to the scent stations. The sun was still high above the horizon, and he decided to go around to the other side of the pond. Maybe something had come along since morning.

The last trap he checked had been disturbed. It was not in the shallow water. Wearing his shoulder gauntlets he felt along the slide wire until he located it. "Something's caught!" he called to Addie. "A muskrat, I think." By then he had pulled it from the pond. "No, it's a beaver! Not the biggest one I ever saw, but it's a start!" He put it into the wire basket, after resetting the trap, and went home by way of the Eltons'. Jess, coming in from his traps, had caught a beaver too. "We're in business at last!" he said.

"At *long* last!" agreed Doodle.

After leaving the Eltons' he met Buck Proctor riding his bicycle home from the store. A brown paper bag was under one arm, a loaf of bread almost spilling from it.

Buck stopped his bike by the side of the road. "I thought by now you'd have made a million dollars at

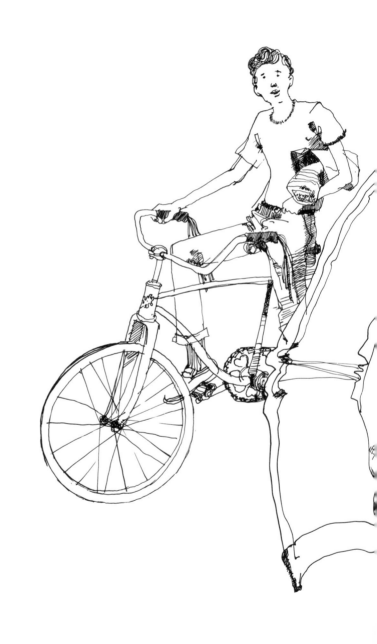

your trapping," he said. "Looks like you'd be riding
something fancier than a mule!" Then he added, "Like
a go-cart!" and laughed hysterically.

"I don't expect I'll make a million dollars," said Doodle, "at least not in one winter. But I imagine I'll make enough to buy a go-cart. Look at what I caught!"

He tapped the wire basket back of him, and Buck saw the beaver. "Its hide will be worth something!" said Doodle.

Buck looked disappointed. Then he asked in his shrill voice, "Why don't you sell your mule for its hide? That's all it's good for!" At that, he hopped onto his bike and rode away—laughing as usual at his own joke.

In the morning Doodle caught another beaver and two muskrats. The country fur dealer came late in the afternoon and bought them, and when he returned two days later, Doodle had three more beavers and five muskrats.

By the beginning of the Christmas holidays Doodle had earned enough to pay back the loan from his father and have nine dollars for shopping. He thought of saving the nine dollars, but Christmas was a time for gift giving instead of trying to hold on to everything. Anyway, trapping was going so well that he'd be able to make all the money he needed before winter was over.

The weather continued cold, and the trapping during the holidays went so well that he had twenty-seven dollars to send to the bank on Christmas Eve. It would bring his savings to ninety-eight dollars.

"I put two dollars with it so you'd have an even

hundred," said his father, handing Doodle the bank book.

"Half of what I need for a go-cart!" said Doodle, looking at his new balance as if it were the prettiest sight in the world.

Christmas
Day

Addie Flowers acted as if Christmas were just another day. She was standing near the pasture gate when Doodle went into the yard, wearing his new red jacket, but she turned and walked away. "I've got a cap to go with it!" called Doodle, as if she were leaving because she could not stand the sight of him in such a bright color. It had been a present from his parents.

He had received other gifts too. His grandmother in North Carolina had sent him a sweater. She must want him to keep warm. Every year she sent him a sweater and something else besides—usually a shirt or a scarf. This year the extra gift was underwear.

He also got a book for Christmas. His aunt in Detroit never sent anything else. She had not been to Georgia in five years, and maybe she thought he had stayed the same age he was then. If not, why had she sent him a picture book of *The Three Little Pigs?*

It was not the best Christmas he could remember: a grandmother who sent underwear and an aunt who sent *The Three Little Pigs* to a sixth-grade boy.

Another aunt had sent him ten dollars, and that pleased him. It would go into the savings for his go-cart. He had hoped his parents would give him money too, but instead they had given him a model car, the red jacket and cap, boots, and a game that was played on a board with dice and a stack of green cards and a stack of yellow ones. When he went back into the house, his father said, "Bring the new game and let's try it out."

Mrs. Rounds smiled. "It's hard to tell which one of you is the bigger boy!"

"Why don't you pull up a chair and join us?" said Mr. Rounds, and Mrs. Rounds laughed.

"I was waiting to be invited!" she said, taking off her apron and fluffing up the back of her hair.

Mr. Rounds looked at his watch. "Or should we go into town first and wish the Carters a merry Christmas?"

"Let's do," said Doodle. "I haven't seen Glenn but once since school started."

"Yes, I suppose we should drop by and speak to them," said Mrs. Rounds. Looking at her husband, she added, "But if Peggy wasn't your blood kin, I'd rather stay at home."

"Blood is thicker than whisky!" said Mr. Rounds, getting up. "But probably by this hour on a holiday ol' Roy's got about as much of one as the other in his veins." He was talking about Aunt Peggy's husband.

The Carters lived in a big, two-story house of white brick, and Doodle was set to jump at Glenn if he opened the door. Aunt Peggy answered instead. "Oh, hello," she said, holding the door open for them to come inside.

Mr. Rounds said, "How are you, Peggy?" kissing her on the cheek. Then he stood back from her. "Fancy coveralls you've got on, Sis!"

Aunt Peggy wore a pink lace blouse with big sleeves and pants that flared out to look like a gown. She did not smile when Mr. Rounds called what she was wearing coveralls. "We're expecting company," she said. "This is a hostess outfit."

"You've got company now," said Mr. Rounds. "Us!"

"But we'll only stay a few minutes," Mrs. Rounds added quickly. "We just dropped by to wish you a Merry Christmas."

Aunt Peggy didn't say she was glad to see them as she led the way toward the back part of the house.

Doodle had heard his parents say they believed she was ashamed to have a brother who was a dirt farmer, as Mr. Rounds called himself. Uncle Roy practiced law in Atlanta, and most of their friends lived in the city. "Happy New Year!" he called from the family room, where he was watching a football game on television. He stood up to greet them, a drink in his hand.

"It's a bit early for 'Happy New Year!'" said Mrs. Rounds. "But Happy New Year to you, Roy!"

"And Merry Christmas in the meantime," said Mr. Rounds.

Aunt Peggy looked at Uncle Roy. "And it's a bit early for being so far under way." Doodle knew that by under way, she meant that he was almost drunk. She continued crossly, "The guests who are coming are your friends, remember?"

Uncle Roy pointed a finger at her. "The guests who are here now are your family, remember?" He laughed so hard that he lost his balance, sloshing part of his drink onto the floor.

"Go ahead, pass out before they get here!" said Aunt Peggy.

Uncle Roy continued to laugh. "They're already here!" he said. "Your family is here!"

Aunt Peggy turned to Doodle. "Glenn's across the street playing with his Christmas present if you'd like to go visit with him."

"Yes, ma'am, I would," said Doodle, zipping up his new red jacket. As he left the house, Uncle Roy was saying, "Why don't we all have a little drinkie, what do you say?"

Doodle hurried across the street. There were no houses there, but the land had been cleared for building. Big trees had been left, but most of the undergrowth had been cleared away. He did not see his cousin anywhere, so he called loudly, "Hey, Glenn, where are you?"

Suddenly there was the sound of a motor starting, and a second later Glenn came around a clump of pine trees, stopping in front of him. Doodle could not believe what he saw: Glenn was riding in a go-cart.

"How do you like it?" Glenn asked.

"A go-cart!" said Doodle, as if he doubted what he saw.

"Of course, it's a go-cart," said Glenn. "What'd you think it was, a motorcycle?"

"But I didn't know you were going to get a go-cart."

"I didn't either," said Glenn. "I didn't even know I wanted one, but watch this!" At that, he spun off. He circled around the clump of pine trees twice and then drove away. Doodle raced along beside him till he was out of breath. When Glenn finally returned, Doodle walked around the go-cart, looking at it from every

angle. "It's just like Donald Moreland's," he said, "the one we rode at Elsie's party."

"Mamma said mine cost ten dollars more," said Glenn. "Prices have gone up. But watch this!" At that, he drove around a big tree and then sped forward through the woods, staying gone a long time. When he came back he said, "Now watch me do the doughnut!" At that, he turned the front wheels at a sharp angle and spun the cart around in a circle before driving off again.

At last he returned, stopping in front of Doodle. "Want to take a turn?" he asked.

Doodle had begun to wonder if Glenn was ever going to offer him a chance to ride. "Well, yes," he said, trying not to sound too anxious. "I guess so." He got in the cart and circled the clump of pines. "It rides good," he called to Glenn, thinking he would take off now on a ride through the woods, but Glenn said, "Hey, come on, let's go inside! I'm getting cold." He motioned for Doodle to get out of the cart.

Glenn got back into it and drove it across the street. Doodle ran after him, and they went into the house.

Aunt Peggy stood at the kitchen cabinet, a ruffled apron over her hostess outfit, putting tiny sandwiches onto a platter. Mrs. Rounds was sitting at a stool by the counter, stuffing pieces of celery with a cheese spread and arranging them on a tray with radishes and pickles.

Glenn reached for a big stuffed olive, but his mother stopped him. "They're for company," she said.

"Doodle is company," said Glenn. "Can he have one?"

"*Other* company," said Aunt Peggy. "Now get out of the kitchen!"

Glenn and Doodle went into the family room, where

their fathers were watching the ball game. The boys became interested in the game too, although Doodle asked twice about going outside. Both times Glenn said he wasn't ready.

After a while the two women came into the room. Aunt Peggy put a dish of cashew nuts on a bookcase and a bowl of potato chips on the coffee table. As she passed the television set, she switched it off.

"What do you think you're doing?" asked Uncle Roy angrily.

"Turning off the television set," said Aunt Peggy. "What did you think I was doing? I am *not* going to have it going when the guests arrive. Now they are your friends, and if you didn't want to have them over, you should have said so. But I'm not going to have the party ruined by a silly ball game on television where the crowd is gathered."

"Aw, cut it out!" said Uncle Roy.

"If any guests want to watch football, they can go upstairs."

"Come on, Doodle," said Glenn. "Let's go play with the go-cart some more."

Doodle jumped up, anxious for another chance to ride, but Mrs. Rounds said, "No, I expect we'd better head home." To Aunt Peggy she said, "Your company will get here soon, and we wouldn't want to be in the way."

"Oh, stay on," said Aunt Peggy, not sounding as if she wished they would.

"Better go," said Mr. Rounds. "See you next Christmas!"

Mrs. Rounds said, "We still live only nine miles from town, Peggy. Come to see us sometimes."

"We'll do that," said Aunt Peggy, which was what she always said.

Uncle Roy got to his feet as they were leaving, almost stumbling. "Happy New Year!" he called, laughing again.

On the way home, Doodle talked about the go-cart. "And at the Morelands' party on the Fourth of July," he said, "Glenn didn't care enough about Donald's cart to take but one ride. He spent most of the time swimming."

"Maybe next year Santa Claus will bring him a swimming pool," said Mrs. Rounds. "The way they spoil that boy!"

"In some ways they do," said Mr. Rounds, shaking his head, "and in other ways they neglect him." He put one arm around Doodle. "It doesn't seem quite fair, does it? The way you're struggling to save enough money to buy a go-cart, and Glenn comes along and has one handed to him. But you'll have one someday!"

Doodle didn't say anything, and after a minute or two Mr. Rounds started singing "Jingle Bells."

Mrs. Rounds adjusted the blanket she had spread across their laps till the heater in the pickup truck could put out warm air. Then she started singing too. Doodle snuggled deeper under the blanket between his parents. He wouldn't swap places with Glenn or anybody else, no matter what they had, and he knew it. But still, seeing a go-cart again—and having a chance to be in it, even though he didn't get to take a real ride— made him want one more than ever.

He was glad his father had said, "You'll have one someday!" That somehow made it certain, and he felt so happy that he joined in on the chorus of "Jingle Bells."

Jackpot!

On the morning after Christmas Doodle said, "Today we'll hit the jackpot!" He was talking to Addie Flowers while he put the blanket and wire basket onto her back. If mules could talk, she might have answered, "Every morning you say, 'Today we'll hit the jackpot!'"

"I told you so!" said Doodle, at the first trap. A muskrat was in it. "You didn't believe me, did you?" But the other traps were empty, and on the way home he said, "Tomorrow we'll hit the jackpot!"

Still, it came as a surprise to him the next day that he really did have good luck. There was a big beaver in the trap near the stump and an even larger one at the trap near the hollow log.

"Two of the biggest ones caught in this part of the state," said the country fur dealer.

"The daddy beaver and the grandaddy!" said Mr. Rounds. "I'll get my bottomland back yet." He was talking about a section of the field he had quit cultivating when water from the beaver pond backed onto it.

"And I'll get my go-cart!" said Doodle.

The weather continued cold during the week after Christmas, and the trapping continued good. Doodle caught three more beavers and a muskrat, and when he counted the money to go into his bank account, he had thirty-three dollars. Ten of them were the present from his aunt, but the rest came from trapping.

New Year's, which was on a Wednesday, the family went to Macon to visit one of Mrs. Rounds's brothers. It was past midnight when they returned home.

The alarm on his clock sounded early the next morning, and Doodle turned it off. His throat was sore, and his head ached. He only meant to shut his eyes for a few more minutes, but instead he went back to sleep until his mother called him. It was the first time since he began trapping that he had not gotten up at dawn. But it was still vacation, and there was plenty of time to check the traps. "You're not sick, are you?" asked his mother.

"I'm all right," he answered.

"He's just sleepy," said Mr. Rounds, and after break-fast Doodle put on his heaviest jacket and thick gloves and left the house. He did not say to Addie Flowers, "Today we'll hit the jackpot!" but she frisked about as if she believed they would. She broke into a trot on the way out of the yard.

Two muskrats were all that had been caught, and Doodle was glad to go back home. In the house, he got out his model car, but changed his mind about working on it. He felt tired, so he put the car aside and turned on television, stretching out on the sofa to watch it. When his mother called him to lunch, he was asleep. "I believe you have a fever," she said, and after he had eaten she gave him medicine and put him to bed for the afternoon.

He felt better in the evening as he lay on the sofa, watching a Western on TV. When it ended, his mother gave him more medicine. "I'm afraid you have bronchi-tis," she said. "But we'll have you cured by the end of the week."

"The end of the week?" said Doodle. "I'm cured now! What about my trapping?"

"No more during the holidays," she said.

Doodle looked at his father. "Your mother's right," said Mr. Rounds. "But I'll check your traps tomorrow and close them."

104

"Close them?" said Doodle, almost shouting it.

"If I weren't so busy I'd check them every day, but since I won't be able to do that, I'll shut them down."

School started on Monday, and Doodle gathered up his books. Mrs. Rounds, making up beds in the front part of the house, called to him as he was leaving. "Make sure you wear your sweater and jacket when you're outdoors today, do you hear?"

"Yes, ma'am, I hear."

"And don't play too hard at recess. And eat a warm lunch."

"I will," he answered, closing the back door.

He was disgusted with bronchitis. It had kept him from trapping since Wednesday, but it was not going to keep him from school for even one day. It did not help his feelings when Jess Elton told him on the bus about catching six beavers since New Year's. He was glad Jess had been lucky, but he knew that he would have had some of the same kind of luck if he hadn't been sick.

By the end of the first day in school he had forgotten that he had ever had bronchitis, but his mother had not. The dampness out of doors would not be good for him, she insisted.

"But I caught bronchitis after we went to Macon, not from trapping," he said, although he knew he would not win the argument. It was one of those times his mother would have her way.

He was not allowed to return to his traps until the weekend. He reset them on Saturday, and on Sunday he caught a muskrat. On Monday afternoon in the trap near the beech tree there was a beaver, another big one. It would bring a good price, and Doodle went to sleep that night thinking about a go-cart. It was still on his mind when he awoke in the morning, and he dressed quickly and hurried from the house.

There had been a sleet storm during the night, and everything was iced over. Addie Flowers was in the barn instead of at the pasture gate, but she came when he called. "On a day like this we may have a beaver in every trap!" said Doodle.

Addie looked as if she agreed and was anxious to start. Yet she moved slowly across the frozen ground when they set out. Doodle did not try to make her go faster. He didn't know if mules slipped on icy trails, but he supposed they did if they weren't careful.

Finally they came to the first trap, but nothing was in it. The next ones were empty too, and they made their way toward the last one. Doodle almost fell, sliding on patches of frozen ground, as he led Addie around a spindly pine that was bent by the weight of ice coating it. Frozen blades of grass and twigs snapping underfoot made a crackling noise that frightened Addie

when they started along a narrow path, so he left her on the wider trail and made his way alone.

The trap was not in the shallow water, and Doodle reached along the slide wire in search of it. When he had the chain in his hand, he pulled at it, but nothing moved. His first thought was that maybe the trap was in solid ice, but he knew the water at the bottom of the pond was not frozen when there was only a skim of ice at the top. He pulled again, harder this time, and got the trap onto the bank. In it was the biggest beaver he had ever seen. "It's a whopper!" he called to Addie, turning toward her excitedly. At that, he lost his balance and fell into the pond, sprawling in the icy water.

Dreams —
and
Nightmares

At home Doodle put the beaver inside the brooder house and ran across the yard. He must hurry.

Because of the ice storm, it had taken longer than usual to check the traps. He hoped the school bus would be late; it was always late in bad weather. But just as he was starting up the back steps, the bus topped a hill in the distance. There would not be time to change clothes or eat breakfast. He pulled off his rubber boots, and water poured from one of them when it fell on its side. His shoes squished as he went into the house.

Grabbing his books from a chair in the kitchen, and sausages and toast from the plate his mother had fixed for him, he called out, "I'm gone!" Mrs. Rounds was in the hallway, trying to untangle the cord of the vacuum cleaner, and Doodle was glad she did not see him. She would be upset that he wasn't eating all his breakfast, and she would be even more upset that he was soaking wet.

The bus was warm, but Doodle was still wet when he got to school. During homeroom his teacher had him sit near the radiator, and although he wasn't dry when the bell rang for the first period, his clothes had quit clinging to him. By the time school was out in the afternoon, he was dry clear through to his skin.

At home he and Addie Flowers set out to the swamp. Most of the ice had melted, and the sun shone brightly, but his head hurt and he was tired all over. Nothing had been caught in any of the traps, but he didn't mind. It suited him to stay on Addie's back and not have to climb down for any reason.

The country fur dealer was in the yard when he returned home. "You know," he said, "you've gone and caught the biggest beaver I've ever seen hereabouts. Wait till I tell the old timers about this!"

Doodle smiled. He started to say he guessed it was beginner's luck, but the thought only went around in his head as if he were in a daze. He didn't say anything.

The money the dealer paid him for the beaver went into the cigar box in his dresser. With what was already there, he had twenty more dollars to add to his savings. A hundred and thirty-three plus twenty was one hundred and fifty-three. In any event, that's what he believed it totaled. He was too weary to look for paper and a pencil to check the addition. All he wanted to do was rest.

He was quiet during supper, not even talking about the big beaver, and afterwards his mother said, "I believe you have a fever." She felt his forehead and then took his temperature. "Maybe you'd better go to bed instead of trying to do your homework," she said. That was not like her, thought Doodle. She never let him go to bed until the next day's school work had been done.

In the morning he did not wake up when the alarm on his clock sounded. His mother came into the room and turned it off, and he awoke when she put her hand on his forehead. "You're still running a temperature," she said.

Doodle got up and started to take off his pajamas. "No need to dress," said Mrs. Rounds. "You'd better stay home today."

"I feel okay," said Doodle, but his mother said firmly that he was not to leave the house. He got back in bed and snuggled under the cover. At least he was getting a day off from school this time.

All morning his mother came in and out of his room, checking his temperature and seeing that he was comfortable. She gave him medicine once, and she brought fruit juices often. For lunch there was tomato soup, his favorite, and egg custard. At midafternoon his father and mother came into the room, and they decided a doctor should be called.

"The Echols close their office on Wednesdays," said Mrs. Rounds. She was at the desk in the hall, looking up the telephone number. "I'll have to call them at home."

Dr. Ray Echols was out of town, and his wife, Karen, answered. She was a doctor, also. Doodle heard his mother telling her about his fever and the bronchitis he had had during the holidays. When Mrs. Rounds came back into the room she told him, "Dr. Karen says she'd better come have a look at you."

In less than an hour she was at Doodle's bedside, having him stick out his tongue and say "Aah" over and over. After she had examined him, she gave him a shot and wrote out a prescription for Mr. Rounds to have filled at the drugstore in town.

The shot or the fever—or both—made him drowsy, and soon he drifted into a deep sleep and a dream. In it, he saw the cardboard sign he had lettered, DOODLE'S MULE TRANSPORTATION, give way to a big wooden one with letters reading, DOODLE'S STABLES. Horseshoes decorated the edge of it, and Doodle stood underneath, more dressed up than any of the people around him, although everyone wore expensive-looking riding habits. Behind him, hitched to a rail, were a dozen horses, all of them looking like Elsie Moreland's quarter horse, Duchess Rose. Before he could tell whether their saddles were trimmed in turquoise, the sign changed from DOODLE'S STABLES to DOODLE'S SCARECROWS, and Doodle was wearing a business suit. He was waiting on customers who were waiting in line. Mr. Jolly was there, along with The Umpire and a lot of other scarecrows, some of them so grand they could not have been put together from scraps. One wore a tail coat that looked even newer than Mr. Jolly's overalls.

Next, Doodle saw a picture of himself on the front page of the *Atlanta Constitution*. He was holding a fish, and the headline read: BIGGEST BASS ON RECORD CAUGHT OUT OF FLINT RIVER. The newspaper reported that it had been caught by Mr. Doodle Rounds, a fishing guide so popular that his services had to be reserved a month in advance.

Then, in the best dream of all, he saw himself riding around Addie's pasture in a go-cart, his go-cart. The course was neither an oval nor a figure eight. It was shaped like a cloverleaf, and Addie Flowers stood off to one side, looking at him the way she did whenever he was in a race. Doodle woke before he could see who was racing with him, but he had a feeling that if the dream had lasted longer he would have seen Godfrey again.

He felt too badly to think about it now; his whole body ached. One minute he was perspiring so much that he was wet all over, and the next minute he was cold. His mother brought supper to him, but he was not hungry. "Try just a few bites," she said. "Dr. Karen said this would help you." He ate a spoonful of applesauce and drank a glass of ginger ale. Then he took a capsule and was soon sleeping again—not soundly, but dozing on and off. He dreamed that he was walking along the edge of a big lake. Suddenly he fell into it. The icy water was over his head, and for some reason he was unable to swim. He splashed about wildly, and no one would help him. Buck Proctor stood on the bank, laughing at the top of his voice. When Doodle awoke, his arms were above his head, waving as if he were trying to stay afloat in deep water. He put them back under the cover and rolled over. Soon he had gone to sleep once more.

He dreamed again, and this time he was being chased through the swamp. Almost to a clearing, his foot caught on a vine and he fell to the ground. He could not get up, and he could not move or call out. Standing over him was Mr. Sinister, the scarecrow, a toy pistol in his hand. Then he saw that it wasn't the scarecrow; it was Sinister Slim, the television gunman, and the pistol was a real one. Doodle still could not move, but suddenly he was able to scream. With the return of his voice came the power to move, and he began to kick, trying to get up.

Someone was holding him on the ground. He heard
someone else say, "It's all right." Gradually he began to
wake up, and he realized that his father had his arms
around him, holding him firmly in bed. His mother was
there too. "It's all right," she said again.

The
Decision

It was the middle of February before Doodle went back to school. When he returned home in the afternoon, he ran into the house and put down his books. After speaking to his mother, he hurried into the yard. Mr. Rounds was sharpening mower blades in the tractor shelter, and Doodle began dragging out traps. "I found where you put them," he explained to his father, who had stored the traps in a corner of the shelter.

"I'm going inside to get warm," said his father. Doodle had expected him to say how glad he was that the traps were going to be set again. But he looked worried as he started toward the house. "And don't you stay out too long," he called. "It's still cold even if the sun is warmer than it has been."

Doodle told Addie Flowers, who was watching him

put the traps onto the workbench, "That's why we've got to go back to trapping in a hurry. We won't have much more cold weather." Addie looked as if she understood.

"Fifty-seven more dollars!" said Doodle. "That's how much I need for the go-cart. If they hadn't gone up ten dollars I'd only need forty-seven."

Addie walked off as if she were disgusted with the way the prices of everything went up, but she returned a few minutes later, and Doodle told her about the track he planned to lay out. "I saw it in a dream," he said, "and a cloverleaf design for a track looks very much like the clover leaves you've been eating all your life." She looked at him as though he were crazy. "But, of course, it's lots bigger," he said just as his father called him to come to the house.

"We want to talk to you," said Mr. Rounds. The way he said it made Doodle wonder if he had done something wrong.

Inside, Mr. Rounds sat by a heater in the kitchen, and Mrs. Rounds put a glass containing three daffodils onto the center of the table. "The very first ones," she said, standing back to admire the flowers. "These are always weeks ahead of the other varieties and probably are all we'll have for a while. But still, they're a sign that we're past the dead of winter." Then she turned to

Doodle, who was warming his hands at the heater. "I'm sorry to have to tell you, but you're not to go back to your trapping."

"But I'm well," said Doodle.

"Not well enough to go back to your trapping."

Doodle looked at his father, hoping for help from him, but Mr. Rounds said, "Maybe next year."

"Next year!" said Doodle. "Why, next year's a year away!"

Mr. Rounds smiled. "Well, yes, I suppose it is. But your mother's right. You'd better not reset the traps."

"But I won't get all wet again, I promise."

"It's the dampness in the air where you set your traps," said his mother, "and staying out in the cold too long at a time. Dr. Karen wants you to be especially careful for a while."

"But she let me go back to school," said Doodle.

His mother said, "It doesn't seem quite fair, does it?"

Doodle didn't answer. Only a few minutes ago he could almost see his go-cart, the one he had thought he would have someday.

"Never mind," said Mr. Rounds. "I've figured out a way for you to get yourself a riding vehicle."

"Really?" said Doodle.

"Yes, I'll give you Addie Flowers!"

"Aw, no!" said Doodle. "A mule's not the same as a go-cart!"

"And a mule's not a vehicle," added Mrs. Rounds.

"Let me finish," said Mr. Rounds. "Remember Mr. Maxwell, the man from across the river who grew up on a farm?"

"Yes," said Doodle, "he bought Dainty."

"And now he wants to buy Addie."

"Buy Addie?" said Doodle, as if he couldn't believe it.

"Yes, he wants to plant a peanut patch and a garden, and he says he'd be happier if he had a mule to plow. He offered me seventy dollars for Addie. So you see, if I give her to you and you sell her to him, you'll have more than enough money for your go-cart." He looked squarely into Doodle's eyes, adding, "It's your decision to make."

"What about your own garden?" asked Mrs. Rounds. "And what'll you use to plow your watermelon patch?"

"The tractor. I'll join modern times and use the tractor for everything."

Mrs. Rounds said, "But you've always said there's nothing like plowing a mule to keep you in tune with nature."

"If I'm not in tune by now," answered Mr. Rounds, "I don't suppose I ever will be."

While his parents talked, Doodle went back to the yard. He swung himself onto the thinking end of the workbench and looked out over the pasture. A go-cart was as good as his now—if he wanted it. *If he wanted it? Of course, he did!* He wanted it more than anything in the world. With his mind's eye he could see himself riding on a cloverleaf track. Wouldn't Addie Flowers be surprised when he appeared in a go-cart? Then he remembered that he wouldn't have Addie *and* a go-cart. He could have Addie *or* a go-cart—if he got a go-cart any time soon. That was the price he would have to pay.

It was a price he was not willing to pay, he told himself. At the same time, something in the back of his mind argued, "You'd only be selling her to Mr. Maxwell. That's not like selling her to somebody she's never even seen."

"She's only seen Mr. Maxwell once," he argued back.

"But still," the voice insisted, "she just walked up to him and let him pat her. Don't you remember? It was when he came for Dainty."

"I remember!" said Doodle, angrily. He wondered if he had said it out loud, so real had the argument seemed.

He looked again at the pasture, seeing the track as clearly as if it were already there. He could see himself riding around it on a go-cart, his go-cart, till he came to the place Addie would be standing. When he tried to imagine himself in the go-cart without her there, the picture blurred and then disappeared altogether.

He looked back toward the brooder house, and while he stared at a pile of scrap lumber, Addie came from inside the barn and stood by him. She stretched her neck over the fence till her head was almost in his lap. The two of them were as still as statues for a long time. Then a piece of lumber in the scrap pile caught Doodle's eye. A knothole in it had fallen out, reminding him of an opening on a birdhouse. It was the right size for a wren—or maybe a bluebird. There was lumber enough in the pile to make all sorts of birdhouses, and with spring coming on he'd bet people would buy them. Maybe his parents would let him try to sell them in town.

Then he noticed a green shoot coming out of the ground by a fence post. It had leaves like a strawberry plant. He thought of the big patch he had found near the trail to the river. When the berries ripened this year, why couldn't he go into the wild strawberry business? He would find gallons of berries.

And he would get an early start as a fishing guide; there were certain to be lots of customers. If not, well, maybe he could plant a peanut patch too and sell his crop in the fall. Or he might hire himself out to work for Mr. Maxwell when his father didn't need him.

While he was thinking, Buck Proctor came along on his bicycle. Instead of riding past, as Doodle wished he would, he stopped in the road and said, "Have you bought any go-carts lately?"

"Not lately," said Doodle.

"Haven't sold that old mule to the glue factory either, I see."

"No, I haven't sold her."

"You won't ever get up enough money for a go-cart," said Buck, his voice more grating than ever. "Don't you know that?"

"No," said Doodle, "I don't know it." Buck began to laugh, and Doodle shook his fist at him and said good and loud, "I know I'm not going to get up enough money for it this month, and maybe not next month either. But sooner or later I will, Buck Proctor, you wait and see!"

"I'll wait!" said Buck, riding away. He laughed as if he had made the best joke in the world. And Addie cocked her head at a funny angle and looked at him as if he were the biggest fool in the world. She watched until he was out of sight. Then she looked at Doodle, who was busy sorting scraps of lumber.

After a few minutes he went into the brooder house and brought out a piece of cardboard. With a big

crayon from the nail keg he printed on it: DOODLE'S BIRDHOUSES. "I'll put the prices here," he told Addie, tapping the space at the bottom of the sign. "People like to know what a thing will cost."

*About
the author*

Robert Burch's native Georgia is the setting for many of his popular books for children. Born and raised in Fayette County, he returned there to live after an absence of several years, during which he served with the Army in the South Pacific in World War II, traveled around the world on a Danish freighter, worked in Japan as a civilian employee of the Army, and lived in New York City. It was while he lived in New York that he began to write for children. His books include *Queenie Peavy*, which was an ALA Notable Book and a winner of the Children's Book Award of the Child Study Association and the Jane Addams Children's Book Award; *Renfroe's Christmas*; and *Simon and the Game of Chance*.

In 1970 Mr. Burch was named Georgia Author of the Year for *Joey's Cat*.